I AM A KINDNESS HERO

I AM A KINDNESS HERO

BY JENNIFER ADAMS

ILLUSTRATED BY CARME LEMNISCATES

sounds true
BOULDER, COLORADO

I am a kindness hero.

I am a defender of animals,

a protector of insects,

and a guardian
of the Earth.

Heroes are kind to strangers and to friends.

I am helpful.

I am patient.

I am powerful.

I am loving.

I fight for kindness when I stand up for others.

I battle my jealousy when
I high-five the winner.

I help others conquer sadness by knowing how to listen.

When I use the power of my kindness,
the animals and the insects and the Earth,
and all the people I meet, will know they are loved.

And the world will be a better, happier place.

And if I fight for kindness, then maybe others will too.

We win the battle
for kindness one
small act at a time.

For Samae,
who is kind

J.A.

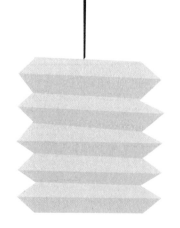

Sounds True
Boulder, CO 80306

Text © 2021 by Jennifer Adams
Illustrations © 2021 by Carme Lemniscates

Published 2021

Book design by Karen Polaski

Printed in South Korea

Library of Congress Cataloging-in-Publication Data

Names: Adams, Jennifer, author. | Lemniscates, illustrator.
Title: I am a kindness hero / by Jennifer Adams; illustrated by
    Carme Lemniscates.
Description: Boulder, CO : Sounds True, 2021. | Summary:
    "Celebrates gentleness and vulnerability in boys and teaches all
    children the importance of kindness"—Provided by publisher.
Identifiers: LCCN 2020008592 (print) | LCCN 2020008593 (ebook) |
    ISBN 9781683644729 (hardcover) | ISBN 9781683644736 (ebook)
Subjects: CYAC: Kindness—Fiction. | Behavior—Fiction.
Classification: LCC PZ7.A2166 Iam 2021 (print) | LCC PZ7.A2166
    (ebook) | DDC [E]—dc23
LC record available at https://lccn.loc.gov/2020008592
LC ebook record available at https://lccn.loc.gov/2020008593

10 9 8 7 6 5 4 3 2 1